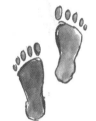

For Coco, who's opened my own eyes
to the world around us.

What Can You See?
Published in Great Britain 2019 by Graffeg
Limited

Written by Jason Korsner copyright ©
2019. Illustrated by Hannah Rounding
copyright © 2019. Designed and produced
by Graffeg Limited copyright © 2019

Graffeg Limited, 24 Stradey Park Business
Centre, Mwrwg Road, Llangennech,
Llanelli, Carmarthenshire SA14 8YP Wales
UK Tel 01554 824000 www.graffeg.com

Jason Korsner is hereby identified as the
author of this work in accordance with
section 77 of the Copyrights, Designs and
Patents Act 1988.

A CIP Catalogue record for this book is
available from the British Library.

The publisher gratefully acknowledges the
financial support of this book by the Welsh
Books Council. www.gwales.com

ISBN 9781913134556

1 2 3 4 5 6 7 8 9

WHAT CAN YOU SEE?

Jason Korsner
Hannah Rounding

This book belongs to:

_____

_____

_____

GRAFFEG

Look at the table.
What can you see?
A fruit bowl, a cake
and a big cup of tea.

Look in the lounge.
What can you see?
A sofa, some cushions,
and a big flat TV.

Look in the garden.
What can you see?
A cat on the grass and
a bird in a tree.

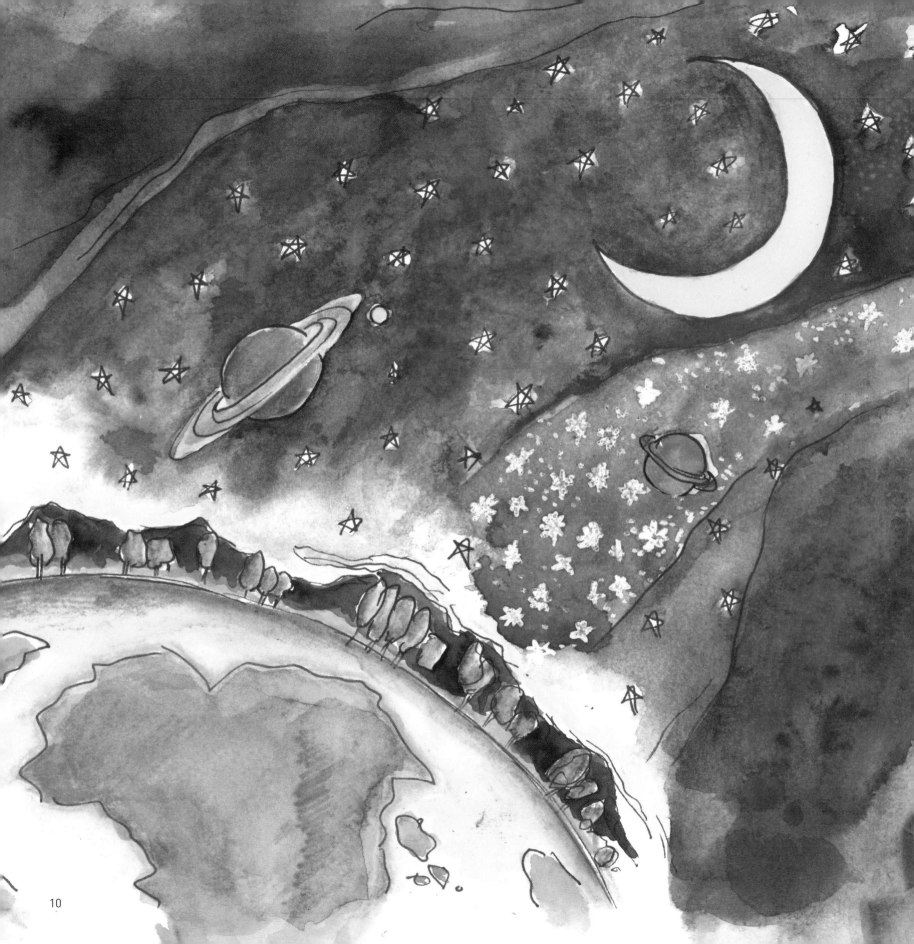

Look at the sky.
What can you see?
The moon, stars and planets,
all bright as can be.

Look in the bathroom.
What can you see?
A bath and a sink and
a toilet to wee.

Look at the jungle.
What can you see?
Chimps swinging, snakes climbing
and lions running free.

Look at the mountain.
What can you see?
Trees covered in snow, children
learning to ski.

Look at the door.
What can you see?
A coat hook, a handle,
and a hole for the key.

Look at the beach.
What can you see?
Sandcastles, deckchairs
and waves in the sea.

Look in your bedroom.
What can you see?
A cot, lots of toys and a
cuddly teddy.

Look at your leg.
What can you see?
Your toes on your foot,
your ankle, your knee.

Look at the dog.
What can you see?
A wet nose, a tail
and a dirty old flea.

Look at the flower.

What can you see?

A tall stem, pretty petals and a big bumblebee.

Look in the playground.
What can you see?
A see-saw, some swings and a slide.
Let's go – 'Weeee…!'

Look at your plate.
What can you see?
A fishcake, a carrot,
some mash and a pea.

Look in the mirror,
What can you see?
A picture of you and a
picture of me.

Draw a picture of yourself